GUSSIE'S

Christmas Story

Robert L. Jackson

Illustrated By
Jan Strock

PUBLISHED BY PENTLAND PRESS, INC.
5124 Bur Oak Circle, Raleigh, North Carolina 27612
United States of America
919-782-0281

ISBN 1-57197-051-7
Library of Congress Catalog Number: 96-71766

Cover design and illustrations by Jan Strock

Printed in the United States of America

This book is dedicated to every child who ever had a dream. For every child who longed to be hugged. For every child.

This book is also dedicated to my angel, Florence. Without you there is no cause.

Joseph F. Conte whose illustration of Gussie will be remembered always.

Rosie, I can only say thanks for all your help.

A special acknowledgement goes in memory of Joseph and Emaline Perry who first taught me how to love.

A special acknowledgement goes in memory of Peter A. Scauzillo. Thanks for the memories buddy.

Hi! My name is Gussie. I'm Gussie the gopher. I live in this house and this is my family. This is my Mom and Baby Brother. My Dad is at work. It's almost Christmas time. See all the decorations? That's our Christmas tree. And do you know I have a secret? Do you want to know what my secret is? You've got to promise not to say a word to anyone. Yesterday I asked my Mom what she wanted for Christmas. She said, "I have a wonderful family and I don't need anything else." But I heard her tell Dad last night about a beautiful crossed candy cane she wanted. She said it meant love to her.

That's what I want to get her for Christmas. But beautiful crossed candy canes are so far away at the North Pole where Santa Claus lives and I don't know how to get there. But I had a dream of a secret map. In my dream I saw the candy cane place at the edge of Millwood Forest. I know I have to go there to get the special crossed candy cane.

I went to see Mr. Squirrel to ask him if he knew of the secret map I had dreamed about.

"Hi, Mr. Squirrel. Do you know about a secret map to the candy cane place?'

"Hi, Gussie. I not only know about the secret map, I also know who has one."

Mr. Squirrel took me to see Mr. Owl. I told Mr. Owl my story and he said, "Ummh, a very likely story, but I have no secret map."

4

Mr. Owl went back into his house and slammed the door. I sadly turned and began to walk home slowly. "I have to get that map. I just have to!" I went back to Mr. Owl's house and knocked on his door.

"Who is it now?" he asked.

"It's me, Gussie, Mr. Owl. May I speak to you again?"

Mr. Owl came out and said, "I do not keep a secret map here. If it means so much to you, go to the clearing down by the old cave. In the clearing you will find three old tree stumps."

"In one of the stumps there is a secret map. You must choose one of the stumps. If you choose the correct stump, no harm will come to you but if you pick the wrong stump, the map will be destroyed and you will never get what you want. Hee. Hee. Hee."

6

Little did Mr. Owl know about my magic words - "Snorts! Snorts!" - which would help me pick the right tree stump. I left Mr. Owl's home and walked to the clearing. As I came close to the clearing I saw the three stumps. I approached them carefully and said my magic words, "Snorts! Snorts!" I knew I should pick the very first stump. I did and there was the map! The map showed me how to get to the edge of the forest, but it was so far away I knew I would need a ride.

Just then, Mr. Reindeer came by.

"Hello, Gussie," Mr. Reindeer said.

"Hello, Mr. Reindeer. Can you take me to Millwood Forest?" He agreed and in a flash we were there.

Right before my eyes stood the candy cane center of the whole world. There were thousands of little elves hard at work putting stripes on the candy canes, getting them ready for Santa. I found the Elf-In-Charge and said, "My name is Gussie." I told him I needed three candy canes and one giant crossed candy cane.

The Elf-In-Charge said, "Gussie, I know you have traveled far to get here. Why?"

I replied, "I want to give my Mom and Dad and Baby Brother the biggest candy cane in the world."

The Elf-In-Charge asked, "How much money do you have?"

Very surprised, I said, "I do not have any money." I began to cry because I was afraid I would not be able to get the candy canes.

The Elf-In-Charge said, "Do not worry, Gussie. You can work for a week to pay for the candy canes."

I was so happy I hugged the elf and thanked him. But then I remembered, "I can't stay now. I am too far from home and my family will worry. Can I work for the candy canes after Christmas?"

The Elf-In-Charge said, "Only if you give me your promise that you'll come back."

The elf gave me three candy canes and one giant crossed candy cane with "Love" written on the bottom.

I almost dropped the candy canes because I was so excited.

Luckily, Mr. Reindeer was still at the edge of the forest. I asked him for a ride back to Mr. Owl's house. He agreed and in a flash we were there.

"Thank you for my ride, Mr. Reindeer. Here is a candy cane for helping me."

"Thank you, Gussie. No one ever gave me a candy cane before. I will take it home now and share it."

14

I knocked on Mr. Owl's door and Mr. Owl came out. I said, "Mr. Owl, I have a candy cane for you. Thank you for your help. Merry Christmas!"

"Thank you, Gussie," said Mr. Owl. "Do you remember your way back home?"

I said, "Yes, but I must hurry. It's getting late."

15

I remembered the path Mr. Squirrel took and I followed it. It started to snow and it was becoming dark. I knew I had to continue on but I was tired and cold. I stopped by a big tree to rest. I had only stopped for a minute when I heard a voice up in the tree. It was Mr. Squirrel. I yelled up at him, "Mr. Squirrel. Mr. Squirrel! It's me, Gussie. I have a gift for you!"

"What are you doing out so late, Gussie? Your mother has been calling for you."

"I just came from Millwood Forest to give you a candy cane and to say thank you. I will hurry home now. Good-bye, Mr. Squirrel, and Merry Christmas!"

"Do you want a ride home, Gussie? My cousin is here with us and he has his sled."

"Yes," I said, "that would be nice." Cousin Squirrel had me home in no time.

When I got there Mom and Baby Brother were waiting at the door.

"Gussie, where have you been and what is that you are carrying?" she asked.

"I saw Dad down the path coming home from work," I said. "When he gets here I will show you."

When Dad walked in the door I said, "I have a big surprise for the whole family." I gave them the giant crossed candy cane that said "Love" on the bottom. "Merry Christmas Mom, Dad and Baby Brother! I love you all."

And that is my Christmas story about the giant crossed candy cane.

The End